You Are Special to Jesus

You Are Special
to Jesus

by Annetta Dellinger
illustrated by Jan Brett

CONCORDIA®

Publishing House
St. Louis

"I don't like your red hair, David!"

"I don't like the way you look either, Jimmy!"

"Well, I don't like either of you because you are both bigger than I am!" shouted Sarah.

"Children, children, what is this I hear," Jesus said as He came close to them. "Are you unhappy with the way I made you?"

And God saw all that He had made, and it was very good.

Genesis 1:31

The children were surprised to see Jesus standing there with them. They had forgotten that He is always with them and hears everything they say.

I will be with you always.

Matthew 28:20

David, Jimmy, and Sarah looked at each other sadly and then quickly told Jesus they were sorry.

Jesus knelt down beside them, took their hands in His, and said, "I forgive you." Then He invited the children to sit with Him under a spreading oak tree.

"David, you are special to Me," Jesus said as He patted David's curly red hair. Next Jesus looked at Jimmy, tickled him under the chin, and said, "You are special to Me, too." Sarah knew she wasn't as big as the boys and wondered if she was special to Jesus.

Do you think Sarah was special to Jesus? Why?

Then Jesus winked His eye, squeezed Sarah's hand, and said, "Little people are important to Me. You are special, too!" Sarah smiled and felt very big because Jesus loved her.

Jesus put His arms around the children and pulled them closer to Him. He looked lovingly at them and said, "You are all important to Me because I made each one of you (Psalm 139:13). 'I chose you' (John 15:16) and 'I have called you by name, you are mine' (Isaiah 43:1)."

"Wow, you chose me!" Jimmy shouted. "That makes me feel important." Sarah and David agreed with Jimmy.

The Lord your God has chosen you out of all the peoples on the face of the earth to be his people, his treasured possession.
Deuteronomy 7:6

"I am glad you feel that way," Jesus said. "There is no one else in the entire world exactly like you. You are one of a kind. My special children. This is what makes you so special to Me."

Did Jesus make you? How do you know?

"I gave some people long hair, others short hair," Jesus continued. "Some have curly hair, while others have straight hair. I decided I would give Sarah blond hair and Jimmy black."

Sarah and Jimmy smiled and giggled. Then Jesus looked at David and said, "I chose red hair especially for you." David had a big smile on his face as he ran his fingers through his curly red hair.

"I knew exactly what color eyes each of you should have, too," Jesus said. Then He asked, "To whom did I give brown eyes?"

The children quickly looked at each other and then excitedly pointed to Jimmy. "Jimmy has the brown eyes," shouted Sarah and David. Jimmy wiggled and smiled. His eyes twinkled. He felt very special to know that Jesus had chosen brown eyes especially for him.

What color hair and eyes did Jesus give you?

"I gave some people a short nose, to others I gave a longer nose. I made all different sizes of ears and shapes of faces, too." The children felt their noses, ears, and faces, knowing Jesus had made them exactly the way He wanted them.

What kind of nose, ears, and face did Jesus give you?

Jesus paused and smiled. "I even gave some people a big wide smile, while others have a tiny little smile." The children all smiled their special smiles and giggled.

What kind of smile did Jesus give you?

Jesus pointed to their hands and feet and said, "I gave some people small hands, and to others I gave bigger hands. Some people have very, very big feet, while to others I gave small feet."

What kind of hands and feet did Jesus give you?

"Jesus," Jimmy interrupted, "did You give people different colors of skin to make them special, too?"

"Yes, I did, Jimmy. I chose a special color just for you. I know exactly what color skin each person in the world should have. You all make My world beautiful."

What color of skin did Jesus give you?

"Wow, You are so smart, Jesus!" Jimmy said.

Sarah cleared her throat. "Uh, uh, Jesus, could I ask You a question?" Jesus nodded His head. "Please tell me why Jimmy and David are bigger than I am. I get so tired of being little."

Jesus smiled a big happy smile. Then He asked Sarah, David, and Jimmy to stand up. He looked at Sarah and said, "You are right. They are bigger than you are. Come and sit on my lap, Sarah."

Sarah didn't hesitate. She knew Jesus loved her. She loved the feeling of being held by Him.

Jesus put His arms around her and said, "Sarah, little people are just as important to Me as big people."

"They are?" replied Sarah.

"Just because you are not as big as David and Jimmy does not mean you aren't special. I have made you just the size I wanted you to be. I knew exactly how big you would be when you were born, and I know exactly how big you will be when you are older."

"Wow!" Sarah shouted. "I must really be special to You! You are wonderful, Jesus, to make me exactly as You want me to be and to care about me so much."

How big are you right now? How big will you be when you are older? Do you know? Who does know?

"Jesus, I've been thinking," David said, "I think it is special to look the way You made us."

"It's great to look different from other people, too," Jimmy added. "I think it's great to know that there is no one else in the entire world exactly like me. It makes me feel very, very special!"

Do you feel special? Why?

"I know how important everyone is to You, Jesus," Jimmy continued. "And I will remember to like others the way You made them. I will try very hard not to make fun of the way they look."

Accept one another, then, just as Christ accepted you, in order to bring praise to God.
Romans 15:7

Suddenly Sarah jumped off Jesus' lap and ran away from the happy group. She hung her head low. David and Jimmy looked at each other and wondered what had happened. "What's wrong?" they asked her.

Sarah was quiet. Then she turned to the boys and said, "I am sorry I made fun of your red hair, David. I really do like you just the way Jesus made you. Jimmy, you're neat! I am glad you are my friend."

The boys stood very still. Then David whispered in Jimmy's ear. Jimmy smiled his great big wide smile. They giggled, walked over to Sarah, and put their arms around her. With a twinkle in their eyes they said, "Did you know you are just the right size to be our friend?"

"I am?" Sarah said as she jumped up and down. She was delighted to know that being little was special, too. She ran to Jesus, hugged Him, and said, "Jesus, I'm glad You made me just the way I am. I like me!"

David, Jimmy, and Sarah all danced around Jesus. "Thank You for making us special," they sang. "We love You!" And Jesus smiled!